Library of Congress Control Number: 2011942251

Tradepaper ISBN: 978-1-4019-3785-0
Digital ISBN: 978-1-4019-3786-7

15 14 13 12   4 3 2 1
1st edition, February 2012

Printed in the United States of America

MY GREATEST TEACHER

A *Tales of Everyday Magic* Novel

DR. WAYNE W. DYER

and Lynn Lauber

Based on a screenplay by
Kristen Lazarian and Michael Goorjian

VISIONS

HAY HOUSE, INC.

Carlsbad, California • New York City
London • Sydney • Johannesburg
Vancouver • Hong Kong • New Delhi

Published and distributed in the United States by: Hay House, Inc.: www.hayhouse.com® • *Published and distributed in Australia by:* Hay House Australia Pty. Ltd.: www.hayhouse .com.au • *Published and distributed in the United Kingdom by:* Hay House UK, Ltd.: www.hayhouse.co.uk • *Published and distributed in the Republic of South Africa by:* Hay House SA (Pty), Ltd.: www.hayhouse.co.za • *Distributed in Canada by:* Raincoast: www.raincoast.com • *Published in India by:* Hay House Publishers India: www.hayhouse.co.in

Cover design: Mario San Miguel • *Interior design:* Pamela Homan

Library of Congress Control Number: 2011942251

Tradepaper ISBN: 978-1-4019-3785-0
Digital ISBN: 978-1-4019-3786-7

15 14 13 12   4 3 2 1
1st edition, February 2012

Printed in the United States of America

MY GREATEST
TEACHER

OTHER HAY HOUSE PRODUCTS BY DR. WAYNE W. DYER

BOOKS

Being in Balance
Change Your Thoughts—Change Your Life
Don't Die with Your Music Still in You
(with Serena J. Dyer; available June 2013)
Everyday Wisdom
Everyday Wisdom for Success
Excuses Begone!
Getting in the Gap (book-with-CD)
I Am (children's book with Kristina Tracy)
Incredible You! (children's book with Kristina Tracy)
Inspiration
The Invisible Force
It's Not What You've Got! (children's book with Kristina Tracy)
Living the Wisdom of the Tao
No Excuses! (children's book with Kristina Tracy)
The Power of Intention
The Power of Intention gift edition
A Promise Is a Promise
The Shift
Staying on the Path
10 Secrets for Success and Inner Peace
Unstoppable Me! (children's book with Kristina Tracy)
Wishes Fulfilled
Your Ultimate Calling

AUDIO/CD PROGRAMS

Advancing Your Spirit (with Marianne Williamson)
Applying the 10 Secrets for Success and Inner Peace
The Caroline Myss & Wayne Dyer Seminar
Change Your Thoughts—Change Your Life (unabridged audio book)
Change Your Thoughts Meditation
Everyday Wisdom (audio book)
Excuses Begone! (available as an audio book and a lecture)
How to Get What You Really, Really, Really, Really Want
I AM Wishes Fulfilled Meditation (with James Twyman)
Inspiration (abridged 4-CD set)
Inspirational Thoughts
Making the Shift (6-CD set)
Making Your Thoughts Work for You (with Byron Katie)
Meditations for Manifesting

101 Ways to Transform Your Life (audio book)
The Power of Intention (abridged 4-CD set)
A Promise Is a Promise (audio book)
Secrets of Manifesting
The Secrets of the Power of Intention (6-CD set)
10 Secrets for Success and Inner Peace
There Is a Spiritual Solution to Every Problem
The Wayne Dyer Audio Collection/CD Collection
Wishes Fulfilled (unabridged audio book)
Your Journey to Enlightenment (6-CD program)

DVDS

Change Your Thoughts—Change Your Life
Excuses Begone!
Experiencing the Miraculous
Inspiration
My Greatest Teacher (a film with bonus material featuring Wayne)
The Power of Intention
The Shift, the movie (available as a 1-DVD program
and an expanded 2-DVD set)
10 Secrets for Success and Inner Peace
There's a Spiritual Solution to Every Problem
Wishes Fulfilled

MISCELLANEOUS

Change Your Thoughts—Change Your Life Perpetual Flip Calendar
Everyday Wisdom Perpetual Flip Calendar
Inner Peace Cards
Inspiration Perpetual Flip Calendar
The Power of Intention Cards
The Power of Intention Perpetual Flip Calendar
The Shift Box Set (includes *The Shift* DVD and
The Shift tradepaper book)
10 Secrets for Success and Inner Peace Cards
10 Secrets for Success and Inner Peace gift products:
Notecards, Candle, and *Journal*

All of the above are available at your
local bookstore, or may be ordered by visiting:

Hay House USA: **www.hayhouse.com**®
Hay House Australia: **www.hayhouse.com.au**
Hay House UK: **www.hayhouse.co.uk**
Hay House South Africa: **www.hayhouse.co.za**
Hay House India: **www.hayhouse.co.in**

"Forgiveness is

the fragrance

the violet sheds

on the heel

that has crushed it."

— MARK TWAIN

CHAPTER 1

Chapel of the Chimes was a one-story beige brick building that looked as if it had once been a bank—there was even a drive-through window, boarded up now, that Ryan Kilgore noticed as he drove around the lot.

He pretended to be searching for a parking spot, but he was actually biding his time. He'd been driving for hours, fueled by some terrible adrenaline. But now that he had arrived, acid filled his stomach, and he was uncertain whether he should even go inside. What he really wanted to do was find a bench and enjoy the warmth of the late summer sun, but there was no time for that now.

At 45, Ryan was lean and clean shaven, with close-cropped silvery blond hair and icy blue eyes that had a melancholy cast. People were always telling him, "Smile, it can't be that bad!" But from

Ryan's point of view, they didn't know what they were talking about.

He'd already been in this small Michigan town, a suburb of Detroit, for nearly an hour, searching for a coffee shop after spending the night in a cheap hotel room on the interstate. There was nowhere open for coffee except for a McDonald's, a site forbidden by his young son, Logan, who knew exactly how many grams of fat were in a Big Mac. But, desperate for caffeine and salt, Ryan joined the snailing drive-through line, and in an act of desperation, ordered a large coffee, an Egg McMuffin, and hash browns. He wolfed them down in the car, engine still running, dripping grease on his pants. Then, having hidden the bag and the coffee cup under his seat, as if they were drug paraphernalia, he returned to the chapel parking lot, which he had already driven through three times.

When he'd finally parked, Ryan sat inside the car with his windows down, watching elderly mourners inch toward the chapel, canes and walkers in tow. The men wore ill-fitting suits that left in their wake the scent of cedar and mothballs. The women, wide-hipped with doughy faces and tinted glasses, wore floral dresses with little jackets or vast pantsuits with brass buttons, the kind of clothing he remembered from attending church as a child.

Before he got out of the car, Ryan took from his pocket a faded photograph, the one he had

carried around for so long. For 40-some years, this had been his prime occupation—searching for the face of this man, his lost father.

It was a warm day in mid-August, everything tinged with a golden glow. Ryan peered into his rearview mirror and tried to arrange his features, just as he did before he began teaching, mimicking a look of authority and power. He drew in his chin and raised his eyebrows. But somehow he couldn't pull it off. When he shifted his gaze to the parking mirror, he looked distinctly worse than usual—addled and exhausted.

"Objects in mirror are closer than they appear," the white type on the mirror said, but he misread it at first as "*older* than they appear." He was doing this all the time now, misreading signs and headlines. What was happening to him?

Next to him on the front seat were several open boxes of books that bore his name in large black type on the front and his photo on the back:

DR. RYAN KILGORE, ST. JOHN'S UNIVERSITY
*Amorphous Earth: How We Are Destroying
a Diverse Planet, One Culture at a Time*

A second book was entitled *Data Collection in Tribal Ritual as Expressed Through the Mayoruna of Brazil.*

These books constituted the main focus of his scholarly life for the 20-odd years he had taught at St. John's in Queens, New York, rising from his

position as an adjunct with a desk in someone else's corner to full professor, with an office of his own and a flattering photo on the college website. He'd taught sociology, ecology, and environmental science, but his Ph.D. was in cultural anthropology. The best part of teaching was that he managed a hefty research budget that allowed him to stay in the air and on the road. He also liked the prestige; he used the title "Dr." at every opportunity and enjoyed it when people mistook him for a medical doctor, an error he never corrected.

So far, the books he'd written had found only the smallest audience. These were mainly his own students, since he'd made the books required texts for his classes. This may not have been the best form, but he'd done it anyway—just for the thrill of walking into a room and seeing 20 people seated with a book that had his name in large type across the front.

It seemed no one else wanted to spend time contemplating the superiority of obscure tribal groups. But this was just the kind of topic that excited Ryan—how civilization would soon collapse if humans did not recognize the power of ancient knowledge. This was not one of the most compelling conversation starters, according to his wife, Sophie, who during their ten years of marriage had developed the long-suffering look that he remembered from past girlfriends.

Ryan's hope, optimistic as it seemed now, was that once his books were privately printed, some

publisher would emerge and snap them up. This had been the conventional wisdom of several associate professors in the university department where he taught, and he had adopted it himself.

But this had never happened. He had two closets full of books that perhaps 50 people had read. He had the vague notion that he might give a copy to his father, who would—what? Be completely bowled over and overwhelmed by the talent of his abandoned son? This fantasy seemed too pathetic to imagine. Ryan threw a towel over the boxes, as if to hide them even from himself.

His cell phone rang, and he looked down; it was Sophie. When he'd left yesterday, she had been in the elaborate preplanning stages of Logan's ninth birthday party—and she probably wanted to complain about his "lack of involvement." He ignored the call, stuffing the phone back into his pocket. He'd deal with it later; he had enough on his plate as it was.

Ryan looked at the faded photo of his father again. At the time it was taken, he'd been a big man in his 50s, handsome in a battered way, as if his very features had been eroded by constant weather. He was standing by a truck in a white cowboy hat, looking out with a belligerent stare. This was Robert Kilgore, the man who had walked out on Ryan and his family.

There were many stories of where his father had gone and what he'd been doing over the years—culled from bits and pieces of overheard

conversations and extensive fantasy sessions that Ryan and his brothers entered into as children.

One possibility was that Robert had criss-crossed the country working for fairs and carnivals; other rumors had him toiling on horse farms in the Midwest, in gravel pits, in salmon-canning plants in the West. "I bet he's a pilot," Dave, Ryan's older brother, had said, as the boys sat together. "He probably works for TWA or one of those big companies. You get to fly free anywhere in the world."

"I think he's in law enforcement," Jim, the eldest brother, had tried. "Probably undercover. Maybe for drugs. I'll bet he has one of those holsters you wear under your jacket."

These all sounded equally implausible to Ryan, who had a hard time imagining his father performing work of any kind. But there were certain meager facts that he heard repeatedly—that his father had a hair-trigger temper, a jealous streak, and a fondness for gin—that seemed believable to him. For years, his mother had refused to speak about him, except to verify that he'd deserted them.

Now Ryan took a deep breath and got out of the car and walked to the funeral-home entrance. Inside the chapel, the air was chilled, and there were thick pale carpets and muted organ music. In separate viewing rooms with names like Tranquillity and Serenity, small, hushed herds of people mingled together or sat in folding chairs. Most chapels had a movie screen where images of the

deceased flashed in a loop. Ryan peeked into one where the birth, graduation, and marriage photos of a man laid out in a gray suit repeated themselves in a silent homage that no one seemed to be viewing.

Ryan's grandmother had none of this. As he entered the Tranquillity suite, Ryan saw a bulletin board where only a few faded Polaroids were thumbtacked. Her service was already in progress, and he kept his head low, anxious to remain unnoticed.

Up front, behind a display of flickering candles, a minister was speaking in solemn tones about redemption, maternal fidelity, and piousness, giving the strong impression that he was talking about a generic old woman whom he'd never met.

Ryan picked up a program from a flushed female usher with a brunette flip, a white ruffled blouse, and hoop earrings, who gave him the once-over, as if she might know who he was. *At Peace!* the program read, with a motif of lilies and a smudged photo of a woman whose face nearly knocked him to his knees.

Anne Mary Kilgore. It was a head shot, probably a church photo. Her pale face, lined with wrinkles, looked out at the camera with a sour expression. *This is who I am*, the photo seemed to say. *Take it or leave it.* Ryan sat down abruptly in a back row.

So here she was again, his father's mother, whom he hadn't seen in the flesh for over 40 years. She had been at a picnic his mother had taken him

to shortly after his father had abandoned them, as if to provide him with some sort of family. He remembered Anne Mary as bitter and lean, hardly the kind of grandmother he had hoped for. Hugging her had been like wrapping his arms around baling wire.

What was there to say about Anne Mary Kilgore's life? Not much, according to this church bulletin, except her date of birth and marriage and a list of her children—the second being Ryan's vanished, ne'er-do-well father.

Gram Anne was on display at the front of the room, her battered face visible even from the back, resting in an elaborate coffin befitting royalty. Ryan stood and shuffled in a line down the aisle, taking it all in. The room was filled with displays of flowers rarely seen in nature, let alone in such combinations: fiery gladiolas, clove-scented carnations, and waxen lilies with a cloying sweetness. Ryan's stomach roiled with that morning's coffee and greasy food.

The casket itself looked as if it were the most deluxe of all models—lined in satin and constructed of some titaniumlike material, a spaceship designed to propel Gram Anne to another world.

Who had paid for all this and why, for a woman who surely never encountered real satin in all her life? If Ryan remembered correctly, his grandmother wore housedresses and aprons and scuffed shoes.

Why hadn't someone bought her a fur coat or flowers while she had been living, when she could have enjoyed it? What was the point of swaddling her in satin now—for eternity or whatever came next?

He stopped himself. This is what Sophie said he always did whenever he approached deep feeling—distracted himself with irony and intellectual arguments.

"You act like everyone's straight out of your anthropology books—like they don't have anything to do with you."

"I don't know what you're talking about," Ryan said coolly.

"Ha," she said. "There it is again. You're superior about everything. You think you've got everybody categorized and that you're better."

"That's ridiculous!" Ryan said, but he couldn't convince her, and eventually he stopped trying.

In fact, even his wife would have been surprised to discover how little he really thought of himself, how much insecurity lurked underneath his pompous exterior, how much his craving for reassurance fueled his need to prove his point, to get the last word.

Ryan realized that he must have cousins and nephews and great-aunts all over this room. But the truth was, he didn't care about seeing any of them—he had only one face in mind. If he couldn't see his father, he didn't want to see anyone. Except his grandmother, gone now, after 89

years of what he was sure had been a hard and disappointing life.

Ryan stood in front of her—the frozen visage, the folded hands of Gram Anne. She was wearing a silky blue dress, a cross, and pearl earrings. Only her top half was visible; the bottom part was covered, as if it were too devastated—or delicate—to be shown.

Her face had softened with time, though it still looked angry, as if someone had taken a knife and etched unhappiness into her very flesh.

No matter what he felt, this woman was his blood; her DNA was proof that his father had existed. She'd been made up by the undertaker with a crown of stiff gray curls and a careless swipe of pink lipstick, her cheeks plumped up by some substance Ryan couldn't bear to imagine. Alone for a moment, he reached out and touched her arm, then wished he hadn't. It felt like cool concrete, hard underneath and overlaid with a freezing layer of skin. What was life, after all, but warmth and blood?

He closed his eyes. "Hi, Gram," some old part of him whispered, as if he expected her to leap up in response. He opened his eyes again, and she looked more unhappy and terrifying than ever.

He turned away and nervously scanned the crowd as he walked by a heart-shaped display of yellow roses that spelled out *Mother*. Obviously, he should have sent flowers.

He had the sense of being observed by someone or something slightly above him—a kind of security camera in the sky. It was the same sensation he had when he was in a dressing room trying on clothes. His gaze roamed up and around the rafters of the chapel. Nothing.

In the first aisle of a side row, Ryan spotted the back of a large gray-haired man who was fussing with the program. Ryan looked again at the photograph of his father. Could this be him?

He moved closer, trying to get a better view. What would he do if this were his father after all this time? What would he say? Would he make a scene, humiliating him for the pain and suffering he'd caused? Or would he break down in tears, unable to speak or hide his anger and longing?

He wouldn't find any answers to these questions today.

The man shifted his head, and Ryan saw his crowded features and small dark eyes. Not him, once again.

Ryan continued to scan the crowd as people began to leave.

His eyes fell on a woman on the other side of the aisle. She looked to be in her 60s, with short, feathered hair, a trim figure, and warm eyes that flashed recognition at his face. She smiled faintly. It was Dorothy Stouten, his father's younger sister. Too emotional to speak to anyone, Ryan quickly turned and headed out of the chapel doors, back toward his car.

Dorothy came up from behind him in the parking lot.

"Ryan, is that you? Wait!"

He stopped and turned to face her.

"I almost didn't recognize you," she said.

Even through his grief, Ryan managed to be offended. What did she mean by that? Surely he was in better shape than most of the other men here, with their bulging guts hanging over their white belts, cigarette packs visible in their pockets.

For 20 years, Ryan had worked out in the college gym as if in preparation for some calamity for which he would have to be fit. He had once believed this provided him with immunity and optimal health, and had not even told Sophie the truth—that for all his exercise, his last physical had showed sky-high cholesterol and elevated triglycerides.

"How could that *be?*" he asked his doctor.

"So much is hereditary," the doctor had said, just the thing Ryan didn't want to hear. The doctor had no idea how poisonous such words were for him. He may have wanted to locate his father, but that didn't mean he wanted to possess a single one of his traits.

In fact, everything he had done in his life so far—every backbreaking job he'd held in high school, every class he'd taken for his advanced degrees, every dollar he'd saved in his 401(k)—was all in opposition to his father, to prove that he wasn't shiftless and irresponsible, but enlightened and educated. Ryan

prided himself on his academic career, his fidelity to Sophie, his money-management skills, and his parenting, which was firm but never what he considered abusive. Sure, he had other traits that were not so admirable. Sophie was glad to remind him of them: he was impatient, irritable, and dismissive. But who was perfect? He was doing the best he could with the cards he'd been dealt. Wasn't he?

Dorothy's words interrupted his thoughts.

"We had no idea you'd be here, honey," Dorothy continued. "Everyone's coming to the house afterward. Why don't you stop by?"

"I'm sorry, Aunt Dorothy. Thanks, but I really can't. I just came by to pay my respects."

There was no reason why he couldn't go back to the house—in fact, that was exactly what he should do, given that he'd driven six hours to arrive in this godforsaken town. But her comment about not recognizing him had completely deflated him.

"Well, your grandmother would be glad to know you came all that way to be here," Dorothy said. "That's what's important."

Beyond Dorothy, the church doors opened. A wave of anxiety passed over Ryan, but then faded as he saw it was only a teenage girl.

Ryan swallowed and looked at Dorothy. He had to ask. "My father isn't here, is he? I haven't seen him anywhere."

Dorothy looked at him with sympathy. Presumably she'd had her own heartaches regarding her brother.

"No, he's not here. Is that why you came?"

"Well, I thought maybe even he'd have the decency to show up for his own mother's funeral. I should have known better."

Dorothy gave a sad chuckle. "He's probably afraid, you know?"

"Afraid of what? What the hell does he have to be afraid of?"

"Seeing you, for one."

"Like he'd even recognize me," Ryan said.

"Or your brothers," Dorothy continued. "Or even worse, your mom."

"He should be afraid of that. She'd have him in jail so fast."

"How's she doing, by the way?"

Ryan stood there, as conflicting words warred in his head. He didn't want to tell the truth—that his mother, married again, was probably as bad off as she'd ever been. "Pretty good," he lied. "Better off than when she was trying to take care of us with no money."

"What would you have done if he *had* been here?" Dorothy asked.

"I'm not sure, exactly. Talked to him, I guess."

She looked at him as if she didn't believe a word. "Really? About what?"

Her curiosity was getting on his nerves. "Plenty, believe me." He scrutinized her face for a moment. "Do you know where he is now?"

She shook her head but avoided his eyes.

They stood together in silence as a stream of newcomers passed by, mostly older women carrying foil-covered pans. Ryan thought there must have been three or four funerals going on at the same time. The mingled smell of macaroni and cheese and meat loaf drifted over. The scent took him back to a brief spell of childhood potlucks before he had been placed in a foster home, before his real family had disintegrated.

Dorothy said, "I'm glad you came, Ryan, even if you can't stay. You know, no one in the family has had any contact with your father in years. Maybe it's best that way. For everyone."

"In other words, you know where he is, but you're not going to tell me? Okay, I get it." He turned and yanked open his car door.

"Wait a minute. Hold on." Dorothy sighed, as if making some private decision. "Last time I had any contact with your father, he was out in California."

Ryan turned to her. "California? Where?"

"He had just gotten out of prison and was staying with a woman in some small town—Gurn-something. Guerneville, maybe? But that was years ago. Probably seven or eight. Who knows where he is by now."

"Why was he in jail?"

Dorothy looked away. "Assault and battery, I think. He always did have a tendency to take his anger out on women. At least that's what I heard."

Ryan paced around, trying to calm down. Dorothy's information was no real surprise, yet it filled his throat with bile.

The truth was that after all these years, Ryan still couldn't believe his father was able to exist without having made some kind of contact with him. One of Ryan's frequent pastimes was trying to figure out whether there was anything in Robert's early life that might explain or prefigure his failure and abandonment. Had he been abused or ignored? But no one could tell him. Even Dorothy didn't seem to know.

"Well, our dad drank, and Mom was pretty remote, but they took care of us," she said when he asked her. "They were always there, though they weren't that involved. Other than that, there's really nothing special."

"All the other kids turned out pretty well, didn't they?" Ryan asked.

"No one but your dad ever went to jail or even got divorced. I wouldn't say we're the happiest people on earth, but we're pretty normal."

If his father's sister couldn't give him any insight, who in the world ever could?

"Listen, I'm sorry if I've been rude to you," Ryan said now. "I just wish—"

Dorothy held up her hand. "I know. Despite all the horrible things he did, he's my brother, remember? I have my own hurt feelings." She touched his arm. "Take care of yourself, honey."

"I will." Ryan got into his car, then opened the window. "It's nice to see you, Aunt Dorothy. I hope it'll be under happier circumstances next time."

He started the car and pulled away quickly.

The horrible things he did. The words replayed in his mind as he sped away, merging onto the highway. He didn't know what Dorothy meant by this, but as far as Ryan was concerned, his father had committed just one unforgivable sin—walking out on his wife and family. This was the main transgression from which all other tragedies flowed— his mother's ill health and her relinquishment of Ryan and his brothers into foster care when she could no longer take care of them on her own.

He and his siblings had been divvied up into different homes, his two brothers into one, he in another. Ryan had the misfortune of ending up with the odious Loseys—an unemployed machinist and his wife.

They lived in a split-level, two-bedroom house on a dead-end street near the railroad tracks. Ryan shared a room with four other foster children,

sleeping on one small, dirty mattress. To make matters worse, the house was cold in the winter and broiling hot in the summer; the roof leaked; and there was always a horrible stench—of dirty feet, mildew, sewage, and mice.

It would take years for Ryan to realize that the Loseys were grifters whose prime occupation was collecting foster children for the payments they received from social services each month.

But you would have never known this from the display Mrs. "Peg" Losey put on whenever they went out in public: she would grip their arms and pet them and call them "sweetheart." The real reason for this was that she could never remember their names.

But in private, it was a different story. Brown bottles of ale filled the icebox, and there was a much-used belt hanging on a nail in the kitchen for when they "misbehaved." The Loseys liked to drink and play cards, parking the children in front of a wavering black-and-white TV with bottles of cola and bags of Cheez Doodles.

Ryan had grown attached to one of his foster brothers, Kenny, a short boy with a speech impediment who liked to make model airplanes. He and Ryan used to talk at night about what they would do when they grew up; Kenny wanted to be a racecar driver. But Kenny was only with the Loseys for a few months before he mysteriously disappeared, never to be heard from again. Ryan wrote him a letter, his first ever, but it sat on the telephone table for months, gathering dust. Mrs. Losey had promised to mail it,

but she never did, and eventually someone threw it out. After that, Ryan never got close to another so-called sibling again. He remembered little about the revolving roster of other children, except that they were miserable creatures whose mouths were ringed with orange from eating bag after bag of cheese snacks in lieu of breakfast and lunch.

The forlorn years he spent with the Loseys went a long way in forming Ryan's personality, creating a major wound that had never healed. He couldn't bear to talk about the indignities of his life as a foster child, even with a therapist—how would he start? But these privations had created an ambition in him, a drive to succeed. He vowed that he would never be beholden to anyone, that he would accrue the credentials and education that would ensure that he was always self-sufficient and successful.

He tried to place the assorted traumas of his foster life in a compartment, shut a door, and roll a rock in front of it. Still they rose up sometimes at the most inopportune moments, memories so painful that he felt they must have happened in a dream, or to someone else.

They swept over him now, on the interstate as he headed west—this ride was probably too long to make alone. There were too many ghosts in the car with him.

He thought again of the chilly nights when he'd never had enough blankets, the sparse food allotments that had kept him with an ache of

hunger so strong that whenever he was alone, he'd open the refrigerator and stuff anything he found into his mouth—mayonnaise, margarine, cornstarch—just to fill himself up. The beatings Mr. Losey might give at any time, for reasons that were never clear. What had he done wrong? Talked back, talked loudly, not talked at all? But mostly it was the utter loneliness; no one anywhere to whom he really belonged, no caregiver who gazed at him with love or pride.

He never considered taking revenge on the awful Loseys. He was simply glad to never see them again after his mother, a frayed version of herself, arrived at the door when he was seven, picking him up after five years as if it had only been five days.

"I think you've got something of mine," she said to Mrs. Losey, who laughed out loud at the casualness of the comment.

But by then Ryan had learned how to survive on his own—or so he liked to tell himself. He dove deep into inner reservoirs of resourcefulness and ambition. He lived in books and made a little home for himself at the public library, where he plowed through every volume of *World Book* and *Encyclopaedia Britannica,* looking at the illustrations when the words were too complicated for him.

He returned to his mother's new apartment to find his brothers already ensconced, watching a tiny color TV as if nothing had ever happened.

His mother's second husband, Earl, and Earl's son, Scott, were also living in the apartment, a three-story walk-up designed for no more than two.

One memorable afternoon, Ryan sat in the living room where he slept with his brothers, Dave and Jim, watching cartoons as Earl and Scott walked past them and into the kitchen, where his mother was washing dishes.

He overheard Earl tell his mother they were going fishing.

"Why don't you take the other boys, too?" she asked.

His stepfather took a drink of water and sighed. "I told you. Those aren't my boys, and I'm not gonna be raising them."

"You never said that," his mother replied.

Earl laughed drily. He was a short man, tan and wiry; Ryan couldn't believe his mother had ever married him.

"I definitely said that," Earl replied. "You just weren't listening. As usual."

Ryan watched from the window as Earl and Scott left the house and crossed the street, Scott reaching for his dad's hand.

Ryan walked into the kitchen and stood behind his mother, who was still at the sink.

"Where's *our* dad?"

"You don't have one."

"That's impossible in biology," Ryan said, a student even then.

Dave entered behind them. He was a replica of Ryan, but with freckles. "Yeah, everybody's got a dad."

"Well, you don't."

"Is he dead?" Ryan asked.

She kept washing dishes.

"He might as well be."

"Mom—"

"Don't ask me any more!" she flared. "I got you out of foster care. Isn't that enough?" She threw down her towel and went into her bedroom and shut the door.

No, Ryan thought. *It's not.*

He looked back out the window as Earl and Scott continued down the street. The sad fact was that he would have even welcomed Earl's affection—that was how desperate he was. Their mother may have washed their necks and buttoned their shirts, but he yearned for camaraderie, for male acknowledgment and attention. He had never had it in his life, but he craved it like a nutrient.

In order to get out of the house, Jim and Dave got paper routes, as did Ryan when he was old enough. All three of them avoided going home, since it felt crowded and was ruled by Earl, who had his own mood swings and alcohol-fueled rages. All three boys feared that their mother might fall apart again, and that they'd be sent back into foster care. By the time they were in their late teens, they'd all found reasons to leave home for good.

Reliving these painful childhood memories had suddenly left Ryan feeling guilty. He began to think about Logan and everything he should have been doing these last days. He pressed down on the accelerator of his Honda and looked at his watch. If he drove straight through, he should be able to arrive home just in time for his son's birthday. That is, if he could stay awake for that long.

By the time the clock read 5:15 A.M., the morning sun was starting to creep up. It was far too late to stop at a hotel now, and he was so torqued up with adrenaline that it was clear he'd never sleep. He'd become lulled by the endless interstate highway, by the truck-stop coffee he drank along the way, by the sheer hatefulness that emanated from his AM radio, one furious white male voice after another, using terms like *vermin, treason,*

cabal—words that he did not know were in common use anymore.

And so he drove on, stopping at service areas to eat cheese crackers with peanut butter, yogurt-covered pretzels, and an Eskimo Pie that he hoped would remind him of some childhood he'd never had. But he only felt bloated and ill.

As he drove, he thought of his mother, now living outside Dayton, Ohio, and the last time he'd seen her, several years ago, when he'd finally convinced her to tell him the truth about his father. He had visited her at the house she shared with Earl, although as a long-distance truck driver, he was rarely home. Her health had deteriorated; her lungs were weak and so was her heart. She received disability and spent most of her time lying on her side on the living-room couch watching television.

"You've been asking about your father your whole life, Ryan."

"I know, but I have my own child now, and I need to know."

"Big professor like you. Big important writer. Why do you even care?"

"I just do, Mom. Please."

She coughed. She had never stopped smoking, and years of the habit had given her a chronic hack and a ghostly countenance. Her pale hair had turned white and was pulled back in a thin bun. She looked like a shadow of her former self.

"Well, you're going to be disappointed. Because the whole story isn't much more than you already

know: your father deserted us, pure and simple. I'd just had you, and I was in the hospital, and the two little ones were at home with a babysitter. When it was time to go home, I sat in a wheelchair in front of the hospital with you in my arms and waited for him to pick us up. He never came. And he never called. Never nothing. I was out there for a couple of hours until a nurse came and insisted we go back inside. I couldn't believe he wouldn't show up like that. I still can't believe it, honestly. He never sent us any money. And that was it. Period."

"You hadn't fought or anything?"

"No."

"There must have been a reason why he left."

"Like what?" his mother asked.

"I don't know. How'd you ever get home from the hospital?"

"A cab."

So his earliest moments were ones of rejection and disappointment. No wonder he was so full of rage.

Ryan looked at his hands.

His mother gazed over at him. "You see why I didn't want to tell you?"

That's basically what Sophie had told him—that he should leave the details alone, but that was easier said than done.

◇ ◇

He made himself pull in at the next rest stop and take a few moments off the road. As he was sitting in the car in front of the vending machines, a woman walked by who looked so much like his wife that his throat filled with feeling.

His thoughts settled on Sophie—of how they'd met in a Shakespeare class his junior year of college, of how improbable their marriage seemed now. It made him suddenly want to get back home as soon as possible.

She was the type of girl he had never dreamed would go out with him—from a well-off family, a girl who had spent a semester in a French village during high school, who had her own blue sports car and wore real gold bracelets with little chains that secured them to her arm. Sophie's father was an endocrinologist, a type of doctor that Ryan had never heard of before.

Ryan's own family, such as it was, felt like an acute embarrassment next to hers. But this was exactly why Sophie loved him; he needed her, she said. She wanted to give him everything he'd grown up without. He couldn't resist anything about her—from her coq au vin to the fragrant suede of her jackets. It didn't take him long before he felt that he had finally found something he deserved.

Yet now when he called her, an hour away from home, his warm feelings drifted away. Sophie was annoyed with him, and he wasn't sure why.

"It's not even six in the morning, Ryan."

"I figured you'd be up," he said, coolly. Why was he getting so defensive?

"Well, I am actually, getting ready for the party—but I was worried about the phone waking Logan."

"Oh, of course, the party. How could I have forgotten about that for 25 seconds—"

"I don't think it's too much to ask for you to be home for your son's birthday."

"I'm coming. I've been driving for hours to get there. What's the problem?"

"I don't know—your attitude. You're acting like it's some big sacrifice. As if I'm asking you to give up something. He's your son, too."

"Sophie, please. I'm exhausted. I don't even know what you're upset about."

"And Logan senses it, believe me. He can pick up on your feelings, even when you don't."

"Leave Logan out of this," Ryan said. "I'm losing the signal," he added and hung up.

❖   ❖

In the end, he pulled up in front of his house at not quite seven in the morning, even earlier than he'd planned.

He hesitated before parking the car and going inside. He felt like cooling his heels for another hour, giving himself the extra freedom to which he felt entitled.

For all the years of Logan's life, Ryan had intended to be a good father, while being flummoxed about exactly what that meant. Besides, Sophie took up all the oxygen in the family, with her vast, adroit maternal skills. While Ryan hemmed and hawed, she seemed to always have the right action at her command. She could pick up a weeping Logan, kiss and soothe him, and solve any problem while Ryan was still weighing his options.

From the moment his son was born, Ryan had regarded him with affectionate alarm. Even in the hospital, he worried that a nurse would drop him, that someone would replace him with the wrong infant, that his son would develop some impossible allergy or infection that would blunt his development, if not kill him outright. But he felt inadequate to do much more than fruitlessly worry and drive Sophie—and the medical personnel—crazy with his concerns.

And as Logan grew older, Ryan became an ever more anxious sideliner. He knew there were plenty of things he could have done with Logan, even when he was a toddler—playing him Baby Mozart, introducing activities that increased eye–hand coordination, helping him crawl, then walk. And now that Logan was getting older, Sophie wanted him to teach Logan about baseball, soccer, tennis—all sports Ryan was clueless about himself. In lieu of that, couldn't he perhaps discuss honesty, manhood, sex? But Ryan was more adept at

monitoring the outside world—a terrifying place, full of treacherous highways, deadly poisons, and suspicious-looking men who lurked at shopping malls, ready to abduct or molest children.

"Look at that guy in the blue shirt," he said to Sophie during one of their rare family visits to the mall last month. "He's been standing there five minutes looking at Logan—I think I should report him."

"To whom? The thought police? He's just standing there like you are. What's the matter with you?"

Now at nine, Logan seemed farther away than ever—mesmerized by his Nintendo DS and the electronic world of his cell phone—a purchase Ryan had been against in the first place but that Sophie had wanted him to have for social reasons. Logan could barely lift his head from the alluring video games that would make him—and his generation—illiterate. How could Ryan ever capture his son's attention in order to teach him anything? It seemed impossible. So most days, he let it go—he simply sat beside him at breakfast, sipping coffee while Logan clicked away on the Nintendo DS in his lap. Sitting beside your child—wasn't that being a father, too? Simply *being* there?

Still, there were times when Ryan wondered whether he should have lived out his life as a bachelor, writing his unpopular books, eating the nightly special at the local diner, and conducting affairs with admiring students that he could end

before they got to know him well. There would be no one to insinuate what a disappointment he was.

Without marriage and fatherhood, he'd have no obligations, no mortgage, no terrible heaviness in his chest. Now he could never quit his job if he was bored—or rent a cabin and write for a month without feeling the weight of his obligations holding him down.

Of course, this hadn't stopped his father. But he was *not* his father—nothing like him, he kept telling himself.

He stopped this train of thought as he watched his son open the front door and run out in his pajamas. Logan had a cap of tawny curls and an expressive, downturned mouth.

As a baby, he had resembled Ryan's side of the family, and Ryan had spent much of his time trying to identify who he saw in this brand-new face—mostly relatives on his mother's side, since he knew so few of his father's. In Logan's forehead was his old uncle Conway, of the radiator shop and soggy stogies; his profile was like his brother Dave's; his laugh was reminiscent of his long-dead aunt Lucille—ancient even when Ryan was born— with her toy poodle and affection for brandy. But now that he was older, Logan seemed to have switched and resembled Sophie's slender, wiry side; Ryan felt a pang of worry—what if Logan was too feminine, too gentle?

"Dad, you're back!"

"Of course I'm back," Ryan said, unable to keep himself from sounding defensive. At the sight of him, Ryan felt drenched in guilt and reluctant love. "I told your mom I'd be here in time. Didn't she tell you?"

Logan latched onto Ryan's leg for a moment and didn't answer. Ryan looked down at him and felt a conflicting stew of emotions. He'd never known a father's affection, so he was never sure whether he was responding in a normal way.

Ryan had originally been the one who wanted children, while Sophie had been convinced that she could first become an artist, painting at home and developing a reputation at local galleries. But the fickle art world eventually changed her mind. It was too competitive and cutthroat. She became disenchanted with making art and more enchanted with the notion of having babies.

"I'm good at it," she liked to say; indeed, her labor had been brief, and while other mothers agonized over issues like breast-feeding, she had no problems at all. At this point, the tenth year of their marriage, she was the one who pined for more children, despite the fact that they were both in their 40s. It was Ryan who'd grown skeptical.

He felt that their lives were chaotic enough, even with one child. Sophie was always asking him to do something with Logan at exactly the wrong moment, when he either didn't have the time or the inclination. Was he supposed to stop his own writing project to read Logan a bedtime story, comb

his hair, listen to him talk about his day at school—especially when Sophie was ready and available? He hadn't realized how time-consuming parenting could be. It could take up *all* your time if you let it. But he had mightily resisted being swept away by this singular part of his life.

Because of this, he had mixed feelings about having another child, unless he could be guaranteed that it would be a girl, who would presumably dote on him and vice versa. He had the sense that girls required less fatherly energy and were more vocal and pleasant, that things could go quickly amiss with boys and men, and you'd never have a clue as to how or why.

He put his hand on Logan's head now, as if giving a benediction.

"You're nine today. I still can't believe it."

"It was yesterday," Logan said. "The party's today."

"Oh." Ryan removed his hand and picked up his briefcase. Maybe that's why Sophie had sounded annoyed. He'd forgotten the exact moment of their son's birth.

"Let's go in. Where's Mommy?"

"She's making pancakes and ham."

"Great."

Inside the bright and airy house built in the 1920s and renovated in the 1980s, Sophie stood facing the stove. Even her back was expressive, Ryan thought. In her early 40s, pale haired and slender, with angular features, she was dressed in